D0178375

Barney's
GREAT ADVENTURE ™ THE MOVIE

PUFFIN BOOKS

Dear Parents

This book follows the storyline of the film *Barney's Great Adventure*. If your child has seen the film, this book will help to remind your child of main events and can be used as a starting point for discussion of favourite moments in the film. The book can also be used to reinforce the concept of sequencing. You can ask your child questions like "What happened first?" or "What happened after the egg fell into the barrel of birdseed?"

If your child has not yet seen the film, this book can help your child know what to expect. For many young children who may have never attended a film, being familiar with the storyline may help to make the film a more meaningful experience. We hope you enjoy *Barney's Great Adventure*!

Mary Ann Dudko, Ph.D.
Margie Larsen, M.Ed.
Early Childhood Educational Specialists

Art Director: Tricia Legault
Designer: Jo Carol Arnold
Barney's Great Adventure screenplay by Stephen White
Cover Illustration by Jay Johnson

PUFFIN BOOKS

Published by the Penguin Group under licence from Lyons Partnership, L.P.
Penguin Books Ltd, 27 Wrights Lane, London W8 5TZ, England
Penguin Putnam Inc., 375 Hudson Street, New York, New York 10014, USA
Penguin Books Australia Ltd, Ringwood, Victoria, Australia
Penguin Books Canada Ltd, 10 Alcorn Avenue, Toronto, Ontario, Canada M4V 3B2
Penguin Books (NZ) Ltd, 182–190 Wairau Road, Auckland 10, New Zealand

Penguin Books Ltd, Registered Offices: Harmondsworth, Middlesex, England

First published in the USA by Barney™ Publishing, a division of Lyons Partnership, L.P. 1998
Published in Puffin Books 1998
10 9 8 7 6 5 4 3 2 1

British Library Cataloguing in Publication Data
A CIP catalogue record for this book is available from the British Library

ISBN 0–140–56447–0

Cody put the egg exactly where they first found it. Soon, tiny cracks appeared in the eggshell, and light shone out from inside the egg. "It's

hatChing,"

said Barney with a smile. "Super-dee-duper!"

Adapted by Mark S. Bernthal
Illustrated by Rick Grayson

Cody and Abby Newton were visiting their Grandma and Grandpa Greenfield's farm with Abby's friend, Marcella . . . and Barney was there too! One night, Cody made a wish on a

falling star.

"I wish I could have a real adventure this summer and do things no one else has ever done before," he whispered.

But Cody wasn't wishing on a star at all! It was a

very special egg

that fell to earth and landed safely in the barn in a soft bed of hay. The egg had several coloured rings, and suddenly one of them glowed brightly! What could it mean?

After the children found the egg, they took it to their grandparents' neighbour, Mildred Goldfinch, a birdwatcher who lived in a treehouse with lots of birds.

"I have so many birds that I buy birdseed by the barrel!" laughed Miss Goldfinch. "I bet I can tell you what kind of egg this is."

An old book explained that a 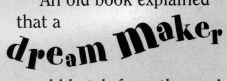 would hatch from the egg! "The egg will hatch when all its rings have changed colour," read Miss Goldfinch, "but it will only hatch on the very spot it was first found!"

"Another ring is changing colour now!" exclaimed Marcella. "We'd better get the egg back to the barn where we found it!"

But in the excitement, the egg accidentally fell from the treehouse into a barrel of birdseed on the back of a delivery truck.

"Follow that egg!"

shouted Marcella. "If you use your imagination, Agnes, we can catch that truck." Agnes perked up and ran like a racehorse, towing Barney behind, as they chased the truck!

During the chase, the egg rolled out of the truck into the middle of a parade in Merrivale! As a band marched all around the egg, another ring

changed colour!

But the egg wasn't squashed! It became stuck in a tuba and was blown across the street where it landed in a lady's hat as she entered the *Chez Snobbe* restaurant!

The restaurant accidentally sent the egg out with a food delivery for circus workers.

Barney and the children discovered the egg being

"Another ring has changed colour," said Barney.

"We've got to get the egg back to the barn soon!" shouted Cody.

They worried that the juggler might drop the egg, but instead he threw it high in the air and out of sight!

Luckily, Barney's old friend, The Collector, caught the egg in his hot-air balloon. Using their imaginations, the friends pretended a log could fly. Suddenly, it became an aeroplane, and Barney and his friends took off!

"Drop the egg down to us!" Barney shouted to his friend. But the egg fell past Abby's outstretched hands towards the ground! Cody took the plane into a dive, yelling, "We have to

catch that egg!

They caught the egg just before it hit the ground as their plane crashed into a haystack.

"The egg's last ring is changing!" said Cody.

"Quick!

Let's put the egg in the barn where we found it, so it can hatch!"

Apple Day King & Queen

"Twinken the dream maker helps everyone see their dreams," explained Barney. "And the dreams you see clearly are most likely to come true!"

Sure enough, when Twinken the dream maker hatched from the egg, everyone could see their dreams! Abby saw herself as a jockey winning a horse race. And Grandpa and Grandma dreamed they were the King and Queen of the Apple Festival!

"See?" said Barney happily. "If we use our imaginations, **dreams** really can come true!"